SEA TURTLES

Written by Carol Mitchell

Contents

Collins

Turtle facts

Sea turtles are the gentle
giants of the ocean.
They spend most of
their time in the ocean's
deepest waters, so you
aren't likely to see one while
you are swimming. However, they come ashore to lay
their eggs on the beaches where they were born.

Sea turtles are close relatives to two other types of
turtles: tortoises and freshwater turtles.

Like a shield,
a turtle's shell
protects it from being
eaten by **predators**.

These three types of turtles have lots in common.

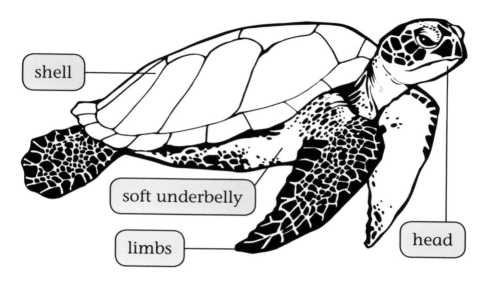

shell

soft underbelly

limbs

head

Whether they live on land or in water, turtles breathe air.

They hatch from eggs.

Turtles are **cold-blooded**. They can't control their body temperature, so they warm themselves in the sun when it is cold, and cool down under rocks or in water when it is hot.

baby tortoise hatching

Turtles are **reptiles**.

These three types of turtles also have many differences.

Tortoises live on land. Their feet are round and stubby so they can hold up their large bodies.	
Freshwater turtles live in ponds and lakes.	
Sea turtles live in saltwater bays, lagoons and oceans.	

Freshwater turtles and tortoises can hide their head and feet under their shell when they get scared.

Sea turtles can't.

Freshwater and sea turtles have legs like flippers and smooth shells so they can glide through the water.

Some can swim underwater for up to five hours before they have to come up to breathe!

Sea turtles

Sea turtles are **endangered**. This is a problem because they play an important part in the ocean environment.

If they disappear, the ocean may be overrun by the seagrasses and sea creatures that turtles eat. In addition, the sea creatures that eat turtles, like sharks, might go hungry.

Sea turtles are an important part of the earth's history.
They have existed for over 100 million years.
They lived with dinosaurs and other reptiles of
that era.

Elasmosaurus

Scientists know how long
sea turtles have existed
because they found
skeletons of sea turtles that
lived 125 million years ago.

Sea turtle species

Seven **species** of sea turtles exist today.

flatback

green

hawksbill

Kemp's ridley

leatherback

loggerhead

Olive ridley

Leatherback turtles don't have a hard shell. They get their name because their skin is tough like a leather shoe.

How big are they?

Smaller sea turtles, like the Kemp's ridley and Olive ridley, only get as large as a car tyre.

Olive ridley coming ashore

Kemp's ridley	Olive ridley	hawksbill	flatback	loggerhead
0.6 m	0.8 m	0.9 m	1 m	1.1 m

Others, like leatherbacks, grow to between 1.8 and 2.7 metres long – as tall as a very tall basketball player.

| six-year-old child 1.2 m | green 1.4 m | leatherback 1.8 m | adult man 1.8 m |

Where do they live?

Sea turtles can be found in almost every ocean in the world.

However, they are not found in the freezing cold waters of the Arctic Ocean or near Antarctica.

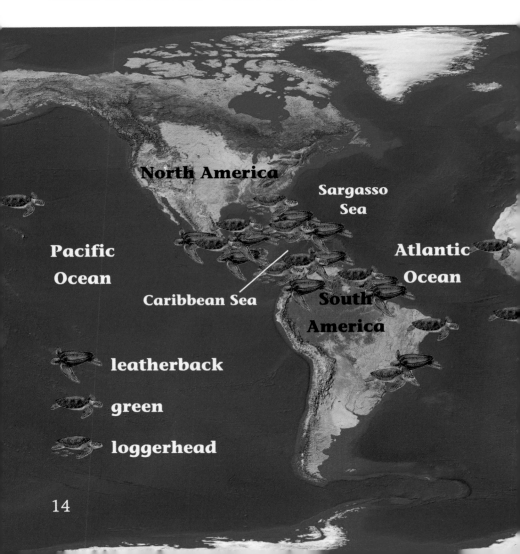

North America

Sargasso Sea

Pacific Ocean

Caribbean Sea

Atlantic Ocean

South America

leatherback

green

loggerhead

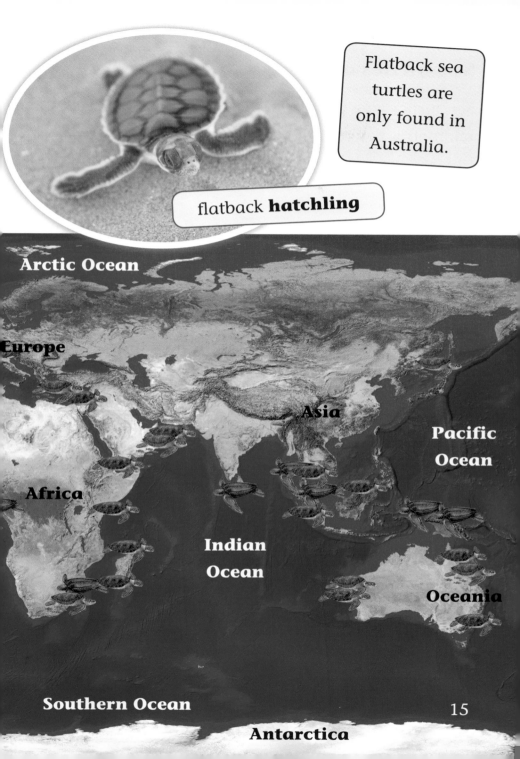

Flatback sea turtles are only found in Australia.

flatback **hatchling**

Arctic Ocean

Europe

Asia

Pacific Ocean

Africa

Indian Ocean

Oceania

Southern Ocean

Antarctica

Sea turtles on the go

Sea turtles love to travel. Many travel thousands of kilometres between the oceans where they live and the beaches where they nest.

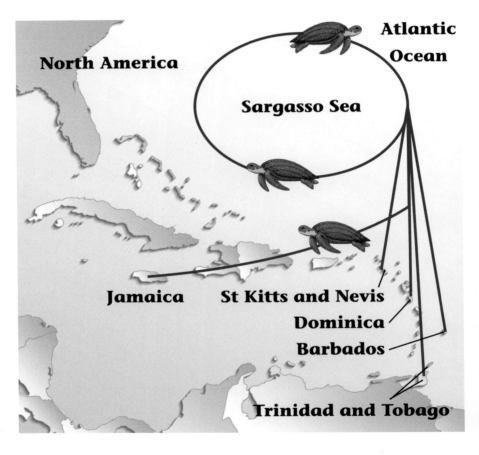

Leatherback turtles that live in the Sargasso Sea swim to Caribbean islands to nest.

Sea turtles don't have maps, but they know exactly where they are going. They can sense how the earth's magnetic force is different in some places than in others and they use that information to find their way.

Some loggerhead hatchlings born in Japan swim 13,000 kilometres across the Pacific Ocean to find food. Every two or three years, they swim back to Japan to lay their eggs.

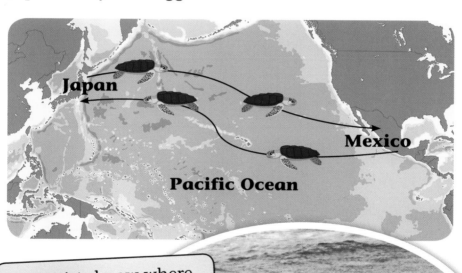

Scientists know where sea turtles travel by tagging them with tiny devices that transmit each turtle's location.

What do they eat?

Sea turtles are picky eaters.

This turtle's	favourite food is ...
other animals	
leatherback	jellyfish
loggerhead	shellfish, like crabs and clams
Kemp's ridley	jellyfish and shellfish
hawksbill	sea sponges
plants	
green	seagrasses and algae
plants AND animals	
Olive ridley	other sea animals,
flatback	algae and seagrasses

Baby sea turtles eat almost everything in the sea!

Green sea turtles eat seagrasses, which give the fat under their shell a greenish colour. That's how they get their name!

leatherback eating jellyfish

hawksbill eating coral

19

Sea turtle hatchlings

When it's time for sea turtles to lay their eggs, they swim to the shores of the beach where they were born.

Mexico

Tobago

Their flippers, which make them fast in the water, slow them to a crawl when they move on sand.

When the sea turtle is a safe distance from the sea, she digs a hole in which to lay her eggs. Her back flippers make great spades!

She buries her eggs deep enough, so they aren't eaten by other animals.

Most sea turtles lay eggs that are about the size of a golf ball.

Leatherback turtle eggs are larger.

Sea turtles are shy and sensitive to light. Turn off your flashlights when you watch them at night.

The sea turtle then returns to the ocean. She won't come back to the beach until it is time for her to lay eggs again.

After about two months, the eggs hatch.

One by one, the hatchlings pull themselves out of the sand.

If the sand around the nest was warm, the babies will be females. If it was cool, the babies will be males.

They shuffle across the beach and make their way to the open ocean where they will grow from hatchlings into **juveniles** (like you!) and then into adults.

When they become adults, the females will return to lay their own eggs.

Turtles in danger

Some turtle eggs don't hatch at all. Humans and other animals eat turtle eggs. Humans may also destroy nests by driving on beaches.

After they hatch, some hatchlings crawl in the wrong direction when they mistake hotel lights on the beach for the moon.

Others may be eaten as they crawl to the sea or while they are swimming out to deeper waters.

Even adult turtles face dangers from humans.

They get caught in our fishing nets.

They are killed for their meat and beautiful shells.

They get sick from trash in the oceans.

They can't nest because the beaches where they were born have been destroyed.

Leatherback turtles may mistake our trash for jellyfish and it makes them sick.

How scientists help

Scientists work hard to
protect sea turtles from
becoming **extinct**.
They guard beaches
where turtles nest.

Sometimes they move nests
to safety to protect hatchlings
from humans and other predators.

They also tag turtles so that they can be counted
and tracked.

All of these actions help turtles to have a better chance
at survival.

Glossary

cold-blooded	animals that can't control their body temperature
endangered	animals that are in danger of no longer existing
extinct	animals that no longer exist
hatchling	a sea turtle that has just hatched from an egg
juveniles	young sea turtles
predators	animals that eat other animals
reptiles	cold-blooded animals that breathe air and have scales or a hard shell
species	a group of very similar animals

How can we help?

You can: pick up litter on the shore.

Scientists can: help hatchlings into the water.

Adults can: ask people not to drive on the beach.

TURTLE NEST
STAY AWAY

You can: make a sign to protect turtles.

Scientists can: tag turtles so they can track and protect them.

Ideas for reading

Written by Christine Whitney
Primary Literacy Consultant

Reading objectives:
- read for a range of purposes
- be introduced to different structures in non-fiction books
- retrieve information from non-fiction

Spoken language objectives:
- ask and answer relevant questions;
- speculate, imagine and explore ideas through talk;
- participate in discussions

Curriculum links: Science – children should use the local environment throughout the year to explore and answer questions about animals in their habitat; Writing – write for different purposes and audiences

Word count: 1,277

Interest words: predators, reptiles, cold-blooded, endangered, species, extinct

Resources: paper, pencils and crayons for writing and drawing, ICT for research, paper and collage materials

Build a context for reading

- Ask children if they know what a reptile is. Can they name any reptiles? Have they ever seen any reptiles? Explain to them that this book will give them facts about one type of reptile – a sea turtle.
- Read the contents page. Model how to ask a question about specific facts in the book, e.g. On what page will we find out where turtles live? Ask children to work with a partner to find the pages where there will be information about what turtles eat, how big they are and where they travel.
- Ask children to look at p29. Explain what a *glossary* is and ask them to add to this as they read unfamiliar words and phrases in the text.

Understand and apply reading strategies

- Ask children to read pp2–5 and to talk about what the three types of turtles have in common and what their differences are.